A Railroad

in

Dearborn

Wissam Youssif

This is a work of fiction. Names, characters, businesses, places, events, locales, and incidents are either the products of the author's imagination or used in a fictitious manner. Any resemblance to actual persons, living or dead, or actual events is purely coincidental.

"And behold, I am coming quickly, and My reward is with Me, to give to every one according to his work."

Revelation 22:12

A Railroad in Dearborn

I

The top of the RenCen building gave way to the sunrays of a bright mid-July morning directing them into Falah Hassan's eyes. He squinted his eyes, knit his eyebrows, and stretched his head forward, trying to look for the next stop sign. Driving at that early part of the morning may not have been as easy as he had expected, but the thrill of his job interview at Kirk's Brokerage relieved instead the anxiety of driving his first car on his own. Falah fumbled for the sun visor—the last thing he expected to check when he bought his car earlier in the month. His fumbling took him so long a time that he decided he had to take a quick look up to find where it was. The look was so quick he was back squinting and knitting and stretching and trying to see the road in less than no time. It would be a while, if ever, before he developed enough muscle memory for more comfortable driving.

The impatient driver behind him sounded his horn and now Falah had to balance his intention to be responsible to drive fast enough to clear Warren Avenue for other drivers, and driving slow enough like any complying good citizen. His 1995 Camry was old enough to catch the attention of others, and it would be a while before he could get his metal plate. Falah didn't even know which paper in the white envelope in his glove compartment was his proof of insurance, and which one was the car's registration.

Above all, he had been waiting too long for this very morning to ruin it with a delay that hindered him from what he had been rehearsing for for the past couple of weeks, and a possible ticket he could not yet afford to pay.

Surprisingly, Warren Avenue wasn't as crowded as he thought it would be at this early part of the day. Falah did not remember that most of those who worked for Kirk's Brokerage, or the other, nearly-as-big companies in Detroit, came from up north— maybe Sterling Heights or Royal Oak or Southfield—and not from Dearborn. In fact, by then, the road was so clear, he found himself thinking that it was too good to be true.

A Railroad in Dearborn

By the time he heard the train blowing its air horn, Falah nervously looked for the railroad crossing he had already been too close to, his hands tightened on the wheel in panic. Was he in his full mind this morning? Did he not hear the ringing railroad lights? But how could he, with the window open and the breeze blowing right onto his face? By the time the train's horn stopped sounding, he realized that there was no ringing at all. In fact, the crossing wasn't even protected by an arm. He couldn't even see the lights because of the sun. His lead-foot slam on the brake pedal brought him to a screeching halt that was necessary for him to barely miss the train zone. That was too close, but thank God, Falah thought, no one behind him honked and no one was watching. He took a deep breath calming his nerves.

The train emerged from behind the old brick building on his left. It had two locomotives. Falah neither knew nor cared how much he would be late that morning. He knew he had plenty of time before the interview. As if angry at him for being too close, the train sounded its horn when the first locomotive was right in front of him.

Settle down, Falah thought, *you have plenty of space and, although I am way beyond the white line, there was no arm so it wasn't my fault.*

The train wagons started to emerge. Falah never thought of it this way before, but the graffiti on them told of deeper stories than the unintelligible coded messages. Back when he used to take the bus to college, he would be too busy reading a book to pay attention to the road. He had never been this close to a train before and now he was almost impressed by the art sprayed on the sides of those wagons. Falah reflected on his narrow time frame: his graduation just last year, his first car he had been saving for, for too long, working for his uncle's lawn business and his friend's cellphone store, his unexpected letter of invitation from Kirk's and, most importantly, his recollection of the driver's ed classes from years ago for that very morning.

Now, however, Falah knew he had enough time to reflect on a further past: the time when he arrived with his family to the U.S. in what felt like eons ago. His struggles in school as a non-native English speaker with virtually no one to help him with his homework. His dream of a better life outside the immigrant community that was condemned to a vicious cycle of illiteracy, poverty and crime. The college expenses he had to work extra hours for his uncle's business to pay and, now, it all boiled down to this morning.

Please, Lord, Falah prayed, *let me get that job. I've worked so hard for it. So many people invested so much in me, and I finally have a chance of showing them the fruit of their love and possibly change* their *lives.*

His train of thought was interrupted by a knock on his passenger's window.

A police officer.

It took Falah the best part of a minute to find where that window's switch was. He flipped it up before he pressed it down. He tried to do that at the same time he tried to put both his hands on the steering wheel. He found comfort in looking ahead by not seeing the officer's eyes.

The officer spoke as the window rolled down.

"Do you know how close you are to the train?"

Even though he wasn't looking at the officer's eyes, Falah felt that the officer sounded absent-minded.

"I'm sorry, sir, my bad! I should've seen the lights but I didn't hear the . . ." Falah began.

"May I see your license, registration and proof of insurance please?" The officer said, and for a moment Falah thought that if the officer had done that before he might have said it somewhat faster.

Falah reached for his right pants pocket and clumsily tried to grab his wallet between his index and middle finger. It didn't take him as long afterwards to quickly pull it out, unfold it and take out his driver's license. He then reached for the glove compartment—slow enough to not alarm the officer and fast enough to show compliance. By the time he picked the envelope, he realized that his hands were shaking. He neither remembered why he was driving that morning, nor that he didn't have to check which of the two pieces of paper inside the envelope he had to take out, nor that he could simply put his car on park and release the brake. All he knew was that his hands were shaking and a police officer was waiting for his paperwork.

Nor did Falah see that there was no police car behind him, or that the officer did not wear a badge.

II

Michelle loved Michigan's few sunny days too much to waste any of their precious few hours—even in this part of the year where her main problem was not having enough nighttime to have her beauty sleep—for any unnecessary reason. That's why she was upset by the time she parked her car in front of her Ferndale apartment. She flipped up her trunk switch and managed to carry all her grocery bags at once. She freed her right index finger and typed the passcode on the keyboard by her building's gate, and waited for the buzz. When it sounded, she pushed the door with her elbow, and went upstairs to her apartment on the second floor. She put her groceries on the floor as she reached for her keys on her lanyard.

After she put all her bags on the kitchen counter, Michelle closed her door and hoped to enjoy the small part that was left of her day. Today had been a very long day and maybe she should have gone grocery shopping earlier in the week, she thought. First, the new director of Human Resources had spent a couple of hours in a totally pointless meeting in the morning, with all talking and no substance. Tom West's move into Kirk's Brokerage was nothing short of a promotion, and his only qualification was that he knew the CEO. It was unfair for the former director to be transferred out of Kirk's only because she had been vocal in wanting what's best for the company. Tom instead gave the anticipated honeymoon-is-over, you-did-horrible-in-the-past, you'll-start-working-right-under-me speech, and although Michelle had already survived a couple of changes in the HR management before and she knew that these symptoms of new management wouldn't last very long, that was still a very bad day for this meeting to depress her for the rest of the day.

Then, she thought to herself, still fuming, she was waiting for the one who had applied for the financial analyst position the whole day, and he hadn't shown up. Falah Hassan was supposed to be there for his interview at 8:00 a.m. so Michelle had to be there thirty minutes earlier, but she ended up waiting for him the whole day. Finally, she thought, it was unfair for the rest of Ferndale to go grocery shopping all at once the same time she had to do her own shopping after work.

After Michelle put the frozen foods in the freezer and the fruits and vegetables in the refrigerator's lower compartment, she put one pack of beef pot roast meal in the microwave and set it to "Defrost" for five minutes. She then kicked off her high heels and threw herself in her recliner. Her hand automatically picked the remote control on the armrest, but her thumb still crept to where the "Cable" button used to be last month. She then remembered she had disconnected her cable service. After a quick look, she pressed the "Power" button.

"*. . . Officer Brown, what do we know about the suspect so far?*"

"*The investigations are still ongoing, we believe him to be a male in his early 30's, grey shirt, red hat, blue jeans, we can't confirm his race yet, as I said the only security camera that caught him at the scene of the attack was behind him. If you know anything about the assailant please contact the authorities. The cooperation of good citizens will be essential in finding and prosecuting him. . ."*

Michelle rolled her eyes. Not another attack, dear Lord. Where was it this time? When did it happen? What was she doing when it happened? Did she know any of the victims? Who did it? Why? What else will happen next?

"That was Officer Tad Brown of the Detroit Police Department briefing us on the latest details about the attack that happened less than two hours ago near a crowd celebrating a birthday party at the Riverside Park. Five are confirmed dead so far while another nineteen are injured, two seriously. This is the second attack in less than . . ."

Michelle's mind was racing between remorse and hope. In one sense, she knew she was part of the system that eventually led to that attack. During the past two decades, Kirk's Brokerage has only widened the social gap between the rich and the poor, between the northerners and the southerners, the locals and the immigrants, which was a recipe for the continuous terrorist attacks against innocent people in Detroit. The

11

assailant wasn't any more helpful in turning any sympathy toward himself, the southerners or the immigrants. Michelle knew that it would be a long time before anyone could be liberated from the tendency to associate those from the southern suburbs with crime and terrorism. It was inhumane enough for all those victims to be killed or injured, it was also inhumane for thousands of innocent people to be victim of public, organized prejudice campaigns.

On the other hand, Michelle felt hopeful that all of these security threats and breaches would not last forever, and that they were a temporary part of what soon would be history. After all, when Kirk had established his firm, his intention was to benefit all with better lives. He did not plan for his company to be filled with the greed of its subsequent leaderships and hence drift away from its original goal. Kirk wanted to benefit Dearborn as much as Detroit and the northern suburbs. He wanted the poor to have an access to a better life. That was what attracted Michelle to his company in the first place. Working for Kirk, originally, was a cause for her and not just a career, a chance to make a difference.

12

A Railroad in Dearborn

Her thoughts were discontinued by the text-message alert from her phone. She remembered that she had put it on the top of the kitchen counter and that she had not checked it for hours. She rose from her recliner and walked toward the counter. Remembering her pot roast meal, she set the microwave to "Heat" for two minutes, and picked her phone. There was a text from her mom, two texts from two interested men she had met months ago, and one from Tom himself that read "ANY NEWS ON THE FINANCIAL ANALYST OFFICE?"

III

Falah knew that he was thirsty as soon as he woke up. It was hot and humid and there was an unbearable smell. He knew he was in pain, but he didn't know where. For some reason, his bed was not as comfortable as it used to be. There was that bright light coming from somewhere that didn't make it clear whether it was Michigan's bright early morning or the afternoon. Did he have anything planned for today? Was he supposed to mow someone's yard or help a friend in his store? Or maybe go to one of the jobs he had worked for months too few for him to remember any of them?

Job. Yes, he had a job interview at . . .

He sat up with a start so quickly he was lightheaded. His eyes adjusted to the light and he took in his surroundings. He was on a wooden bench in a darkened room, except for what looked like a basement window. That was where the bright light streamed in. The pain in his forehead was severe. When he reached for it with his fingers he felt that the blood had almost dried.

He stood, too quickly, to look for a door, and his dizziness surprised him and almost knocked him to the floor before he regained his consciousness. He sat back down, slowly holding his head in his hands. After several deep breaths, he looked up. The place was crowded with old furniture, paint cans, cardboard boxes and a boiler. There was a leaking bathroom that was infested with cockroaches.

Falah reached for his cellphone but it was not in his pocket, neither did he find his wallet.

"Hello! Can anybody hear me! Where am I?"

He didn't exactly feel more comfortable when his screams were interrupted by footsteps coming downstairs. Falah was too scared to rehearse any conversation with what could be his kidnapper.

There was the clanging of a keychain followed by the sound of a clanking amplified by the metal door of an uninhabited space. There was the key-turn followed by a louder click. The door squeaked open.

The silhouette of the police officer from the railroad crossing slowly walked into the room—except that he didn't look anything like a police officer. His eyes were blank and the basement was soon filled with the smell of tobacco and booze. By the time the light from the window showed his face, Falah saw that the officer was not looking forward to this meeting.

"Can I help you?"

"Where am I?"

"You're in my basement."

"What time is it now?" Falah remembered that he was not in the best position to ask too many questions.

"You were going to Kirk's, weren't you?" He also remembered that he had a copy of the invitation letter on the passenger seat. *This won't be good*, he thought.

A Railroad in Dearborn

"I don't *work* there. I was just going for . . ." His sentence was interrupted by a swift slap on his cheek. The stiff slap was too quick for him to immediately feel its pain, but his attitude was changed quicker than he planned.

"Just answer my questions. You were going to Kirk's weren't you?"

A quick "Yes" would do, but Falah knew that it wouldn't sound good. Falah's eyes were so wide open he subconsciously thought the more he opened them, the better would be the infra-red, three-dimensional image he could see, to psychologically prepare himself for any potential threat.

He nodded yes.

"You seem like a good boy. Didn't your family teach you not to go *there*? Haven't you learned what Kirk did to us? Do you even know what kind of people work there?"

In a sense, the officer was right. Falah had heard this before. Kirk's alleged divisions, the gaps in the community caused by the company. Although he knew more about Kirk's than the officer thought he did, the company wasn't very popular in the poorer suburbs of the southern Detroit area. But why did he have to be *kidnapped*?

"Anyway," the officer continued, "You'll be here until your family answers me. They don't promptly answer your phone calls, do they? As long as you stay here nice and quiet, you'll be fine and you'll go home in days. Maybe hours, depending on how much your family loves you."

The officer walked back outside the basement, locked the door and started upstairs.

Falah started to study the basement. Anything that could tell him where he was or who the "officer" was. Despite the heat and the humidity and the stench of a filthy, roach-infested bathroom, and the pain in his forehead and left cheek, his impulse was impressive. He was hopeful that this whole situation wouldn't last long. *Who would've thought we would live in a world so lawless people could be simply kidnapped, in broad daylight, in the middle of a major city?* Falah though, *What could the officer possibly*

18

benefit from kidnapping him, or what could his family pay him in ransom?

The boiler was old and there was no air conditioner. The cardboard boxes held old, useless books and instruction manuals. There were two-by-fours and other construction materials, no longer useful. Everything was too old and dusty to reveal any clue about the house's current resident. This basement hasn't been cleaned for generations, he thought, just years upon years of junk and castoffs.

That's when Falah started to panic. He felt closed-in, sweltering. He moved one box to see what was in the box underneath it, but it wasn't any more helpful. He moved another box to see what's underneath it, before he realized the futility of his search for older articles to reveal more recent information about where he was. By then, his panic has turned into despair.

He looked at his dress shirt and slacks, pressed for the interview that might have changed his life. He was now in a place where everything he had ever worked for had come to an end. All those years studying

Business Administration, working odd jobs to provide for his own college. How long he had been planning to move from the poverty of the neglected southern suburbs to the prosperity that Kirk's offered. How often he had to defend Kirk's before his friends, promising that people had a choice as long as they were pursuing what was right. Now, no one would believe that investing all that time and effort and resources to work for Kirk's was a good idea.

All that aside, Falah thought of his family. It hasn't been very common for them to expect his return home at a time they knew of after being in a place he told them about. They were all just as excited about his interview and no doubt they would realize that he's been late, he thought.

His thought of his family was interrupted by his own cellphone ring, from upstairs, right above him. Although he could clearly hear the ring, all he heard afterwards was the officer's unintelligible humming.

A Railroad in Dearborn

IV

Michelle used her monthly pass to open the robotic arm at the entrance to the underground parking lot behind the RenCen building. It took her a few rounds before she finally found a parking spot at the farthest corner. She was not in her best mood that morning, and she didn't even remember why. She slammed her car door and started walking all the way back to the stairs that started the long way to the foyer of the RenCen building, sighing every ten steps. She took the stairs, then the long hallway, then another set of stairs. Once in the foyer, she took the escalator to the elevators, then she took the express elevator to the thirty-third floor.

Once on her floor, Michelle used the key fob in her lanyard to open the door of the Kirk's Brokerage firm, and didn't check her watch until she arrived at her own office. She put her purse beside her, turned the swivel chair to face her computer, and moved the mouse. She saw a text on Skype from the new HR director:

"GOOD MORNING MICHELLE! WOULD YOU COME TO MY OFFICE FOR A MINUTE?"

Michelle had worked long enough at Kirk's to know that the cheerful intro meant by no means a raise or a work trip to San Diego. She knew that her new superior's bitter honeymoon would not be over for another few weeks.

She picked a yellow file that was on top of a neat stack of papers, closed her eyes, took a deep breath, and walked to Tom's office.

She knocked his door, even though she didn't expect an answer. She slowly opened the door and walked inside.

"Good morning Tom," she invited herself to the seat across his desk on the left, even though he neither answered nor lifted his eyes from whatever he was writing.

After a few very long minutes, Tom put on a show of politeness, wore a smile and stretched his hand to shake Michelle's:

A Railroad in Dearborn

"Good morning Michelle. Sorry I'm trying to pick up the momentum of this place."

"It's okay. You will get busy before you know it."

"Oh, I know, and I'm looking forward to it!

"So, did you receive my text message yesterday?" Tom didn't sound any less cordial.

"I did. I have prepared another email to post an ad at the *Free P*. I was planning to submit it to you this morning for approval. I have a copy of it here."

"Do you have the resumes of those who applied the first time?" Michelle didn't expect that question. She had no idea why Tom was interested in the previous search for the financial analyst position.

"Uh, not here, they are at my office. I can fetch them now if you want." She started to get up.

"No, it's okay. By the way, how is your mother?"

"I think she's fine now. Yesterday she was at a birthday party at her neighbor's house. She texted me a few pictures and she looked happy."

"Is she still in Boise?" Michelle's patience was running low. Tom wasn't obviously interested in her mom's well-being, neither would he be interested in the well-being of anyone in the world for that matter, but she had to pretend that she was free for the rest of the day.

"Yes."

"She must be very proud of you. I'm pretty sure it wasn't easy on her to see you go from Boise to Detroit. I hope she knows that Detroit isn't a bad place to be in at all. Michelle . . ." Tom looked down, as if trying to avoid the look in her eyes as he was getting to the point. "What do you know about Detroit?"

"I like it, I guess. I've been here for four years. It's a cool place."

A Railroad in Dearborn

"It is," Tom agreed, "and I know you feel it's an honor to work for the company that has made it this beautiful. Detroit deserves to be beautiful, but unfortunately 'beautiful' isn't what first comes to people's mind when they hear about this city. I have ordered a framed picture of the old Train Station, to remind me that Detroit had a long way to get where it's at now."

"I'm looking forward to see the future plans for the Train Station."

"That's not my point," Michelle wished Tom would finally get to his point. "The point is," Tom continued, "Kirk had a vision, and you and I are here thanks to his vision. He wanted people here to have a better life. Kirk loved everyone—the rich, the poor, those from northern Detroit, those from Downriver—he loved all of them. He invested so much, worked really hard, practically sacrificed his life when he chose to be resettled here from New York, and now no one even knows whether he's alive or not. How exciting would be for him to see Old Motown coming back to life!"

"Kirk's name stands for sacrifice, generosity kindness and love. His vision keeps me going."

"Michelle, have you seen the news yesterday?" Now, she thought, Tom was getting to the subject, and it's almost the first break time.

"I have."

"Those poor people at Riverside! Celebrating a birthday party and, boom, comes this man and discriminately starts shooting around, killing and injuring people. How sad it was! When will people ever get to live in peace and harmony? Who is responsible for all this? People died! Families mourning! Moms bereaved! Children orphaned! And the fortunate living ones will either be maimed for life or they will never be freed from yesterday's flashbacks!"

Michelle was calmly looking into Tom's eyes.

"I'm sorry if I let my emotions get the best of me. You're dismissed. Go get your coffee," Tom said, gently waving her away.

V

When Falah woke up the next morning, he was too confused to remember that he hadn't eaten anything since his early-morning bowl of cereal more than twenty-four hours ago. He was surprised that he could go without food for that long, even though he didn't need to move much. With all the junk cluttered everywhere, reaching the bathroom's faucet wasn't an easy task, but it kept him hydrated the whole time. He had come to terms with the fact that he would be staying in that basement for a while, and that he wouldn't know who his kidnapper was or where was he locked up. He still couldn't remember how he ended up down here. He could hardly remember his first encounter with the kidnapper/officer.

What *was* in his mind, though, was his cellphone's ringing the previous day. He still didn't know who had called him, or what the kidnapper said when he answered, or whether or not there was even anyone in this whole world who knew that he was missing.

How long could he stay alive without food? Would he starve to death? Had the officer/kidnapper done that to anyone before? There wasn't any clue that anyone had died in that basement before, but again, how would he know?

The wooden floor above him creaked and there was a pattern of thuds indicating footsteps going to where the basement's door was. The creaking stopped and the footsteps continued descending the stairs. *What now?* Falah was scared. He knew he was no physical match for his kidnapper, and he couldn't help but let his fear assume full control over his mobility.

The door opened, and the officer/kidnapper entered, carrying a white take-out bag:

"I talked with your family yesterday. They sounded nice and cooperative. It'll all be alright for both of us. You like Chinese?"

No he didn't, but Falah nodded anyway.

"I'm Stanley by the way. I'm sorry it had to be this way, but I'm sure you'd understand."

"Hi, Stanley."

"You see, Kirk had a diabolic plan to annihilate the poor hardworking families. They say he wanted all people to live better and to have more decent houses, but they were too blind to see that he was only making the rich richer, and the poor poorer. His company only employs those from the northern suburbs and never invests on this side of the railroad. I couldn't let you go there. In a few days you will walk out of this place, and I hope you'll think of what I told you and find yourself another job. You're still a young man and you have your whole future in front of you."

Falah had more questions than answers. How long has Stanley known that he had a job interview at Kirks? Did he know him before? Why was he talking about a brokerage company like he had a personal feud with them? Would he really let him out, and how did the conversation with his family go?

"Your father promised to come up with your release price. He'll call once this happens and you'll walk out a free man. Take a good rest today, don't move too much. It's not good for you." Stanley walked out of the basement and locked the door.

Falah was frozen for a few minutes after the thudding above him stopped, then he reluctantly opened the bag of the take-out food. He didn't recognize the cold food, nor had he smelled anything like that in the past. He slowly stretched his hand toward a hard piece that looked like it was some version of bread, dipped it in whatever was in the small box inside, and started eating.

VI

Stanley had been awake since 4:00 a.m., after he slept for only a couple of hours in his recliner. He had the TV on and he was flipping through the channels. He decided that it was time for him to shave and wash his face. He got up and looked for something in the refrigerator to eat, and regretted that he had given the leftovers to the young man downstairs the day before. There were only two eggs left in a box that he couldn't remember how they got there. He fried the eggs anyway, looked for a piece of bread in the cabinet above the stove, but eventually decided to eat the eggs alone. He needed to go shopping before lunch, he thought. He put on his police uniform, then a rain poncho over it.

He walked outside his house, and was surprised to see an old Camry parked out front. He remembered that he needed to hide it in his one-car garage instead of his own car. He had to come up with another place to store any second car that might arrive later that morning. Replacing his car in the garage with the Camry and parallel-parking his car in its place wasted five minutes of his planned time.

He walked down Chase Road all the way to Warren Avenue. The streets were still empty before 7:00 a.m., except for the sound of the garbage truck in the distance. It had stopped raining minutes before, but he still kept his rain poncho on. He then turned right and walked down Warren Avenue to the railroad crossing, and stood by a dumpster across the street from the Hollingsworth building. The railroad lights flashed and rang and the train soon appeared. Stanley surveyed the street.

A single Altima appeared into Warren Avenue from the underpass on the west. Stanley walked calmly behind the dumpster and quickly took off his rain poncho, put it in his pocket and walked toward the right side of the car as it came to a complete stop at the crossing.

"May I see your license really quick?" Stanley asked the startled driver after he rolled down the passenger side window.

"Where are you going?"

"RenCen."

"Kirk's?"

"Yes sir."

"Did you have your headlights on?"

Sadiq looked at his dashboard to double-check, and saw that the headlights indicator was on. "Yes sir it's on."

"Would you mind if I see them?"

"Sure. I mean not at all. Go ahead, sir."

Stanley walked around the car's front and pretended to check the headlights. He continued walking until he was by the driver. Sadiq lowered the driver side window without being asked.

"Do you have any weapons in the trunk?"

"I don't."

"May I take a look for a minute?"

"Yes sir."

34

A Railroad in Dearborn

"Step out of the car for me if you will."

Sadiq was too confused to question what was happening. He unbuckled his seatbelt and opened the door.

Just as he was about to leave the car, Stanley reached his hand to the back of Sadiq's head, slammed it against the windshield and knocked him unconscious. He quickly pushed Sadiq's collapsed body onto the passenger seat and took his place behind the wheel. He emptied Sadiq's pockets of a cellphone, a wallet, and a card that had unintelligible scribbles and threw them on the floor behind the passenger seat. He turned his left-turn signal on, backed up and then took a U-turn into Warren Avenue, and drove all the way back to his house.

VII

"MICHELLE, MY OFFICE NOW, PLEASE."

Michelle thought, for a split-second, that she would quit her job at Kirk's. Then, the very next moment she knew she would not let anyone take her down. She'd been working for the company for four years already. She had invested so much of her time in this job longing to see her community change for the better. Many a time she was encouraged to see jobs created, landmark buildings restored, houses renovated and poorer people getting grants or loans to redo their houses. Detroit was a better place now, thanks to Kirk's, and no one would ruin that for her.

She picked up her yellow file from her desk and walked to Tom's office. The door was open, and this time he was waiting for her.

"Sit down we need to talk." Michelle couldn't hide her unhappy face, but she managed to stay calm.

A Railroad in Dearborn

"Did you contact another applicant from the former list?"

"I did."

"I thought you said you were preparing another newspaper ad for the position."

"I was."

"What happened then?"

"I had to double-check the company's policies and bylaws. I honestly have never done that all by myself before, so I asked Paul. He directed me to contact the second person in the first list."

"You should've contacted me before the CEO"

"I wasn't intending to take any action. I was just asking."

"I see. Did the applicant show up?"

"He did not."

"What's his name?"

"Sadiq Jafar."

"Michelle . . . you have a good report in the company, and Paul Canty has told me a lot about you. First of all, I want you to carefully observe the chain of command in our company. Making any serious move like this without going through your direct superior is no small matter."

"I understand."

"Good."

"I thought you asked for the first list."

"I have. I wanted to see on what basis you contacted the one from a couple of days ago."

"I have studied their profiles and received their security background checks. I saw their college transcripts. I arranged them based on that and the proximity of each one's residence to the company. Falah's profile was the most ideal."

"Still, you should have let me see the other applicants."

A Railroad in Dearborn

"I'm sorry. I was intending to show you the list yesterday but you said there was no need to. I have it with me now."

Tom stretched out his hand. Michelle gave him the list.

"Let's see Steve." Michelle knew that Tom selected the first name that sounded nonimmigrant.

"He's number *eight*."

"I can see."

"I can't, sir."

"Excuse me?"

"It is against our policies to discriminate against applicants based on their ethnicities, not to mention that it's illegal in the State of Michigan. I cannot be held accountable if anyone decides to litigate."

"I'm not saying we should *discriminate* against our applicants. That's a serious accusation, Michelle. I'm just saying that we should select who's best for our company and community. Didn't you have your first two applicants ignore their interview?

"Michelle. Kirk's is not just a company. We have the stewardship of Detroit. Everything we do will either make or break this city. We need to focus on what is good and discard what's not useful. The city's demographics change according to what we do here. We choose who comes over and who leaves, and we want only those who love our city. You know that each new applicant may be able to relocate here or in the northern suburbs within a year. I don't want those from across the railroad to ruin what we've been doing for two decades . . ."

Michelle couldn't believe what she had just heard from the new HR director.

"I mean, you get the point, Michelle. Let's be wise beyond those bureaucratic routines and choose only those that we know will serve our company and our community. Call Steve Kidds."

A Railroad in Dearborn

VIII

Stanley parked Sadiq's Altima behind his car in front of his house, and scanned Chase Road on both directions. He wondered what school was open for what looked like three schoolgirls walking together in this part of the summer. He waited until the girl took a turn and disappeared out of sight before he took another look down the street. He got out of the driver seat, picked up Sadiq's collapsed, unconscious body from the passenger seat and carried him with his right arm around the body. Sadiq's forehead was still bleeding. His body wasn't totally motionless, but he was not aware of his surroundings and he certainly couldn't make any significant move to free himself.

Stanley walked with Sadiq's body toward the house, reached for his keys in his left pants pocket, opened the door and went inside. He turned left and went downstairs toward the basement. Still holding the keys in his left hand, he opened the basement door and went inside.

Falah was already awake, but still lying down on the wooden bench. He was alarmed at the sight of Sadiq's body, bleeding forehead and half-open blank eyes.

"Either of you make any noise, and you're both dead." Stanley lowered Sadiq's body onto the concrete floor, walked outside and closed the basement door.

Falah stood up, approached the new prisoner, and crouched down next to him.

"You okay?" Falah patted Sadiq, then gently rocked his left shoulder. "Can you hear me? Hey there! What's your name?"

Falah went to the bathroom sink, cupped his hands and took some water back to the newcomer. He managed to sprinkle Sadiq's face with what was left of it by the time he arrived back at his body.

"Goodness!" Falah saw a blank stare that he couldn't tell whether it recognized him or not.

Falah scanned the basement for anything that might work as a pitcher. He went for the construction materials at the far end and saw an empty paint can. He took the can back to the bathroom sink, filled it with water and brought it back to Sadiq. He hesitated a little after he saw a few crusts of dry paint floating on the water, but took some water on his fingers and flicked Sadiq's face with it anyway.

"You okay?" Falah cupped some more water and wiped Sadiq's face around the wound, then carefully reached the wound before he decided best not to touch it.

Desperate, hungry, weak, and confused, Falah walked back to his wooden bench, laid down and continued to stare with curiosity at his new basement-mate.

IX

Michelle was looking at an old episode of a dance show but she wasn't really watching. She munched on one more Cheeto and decided that it was enough for tonight. She looked at her guitar, neatly propped up against a stand at the far corner of her living room, thought she hadn't played it for so long her fingers might already be too rusty to play for a minute, but then decided she could strum it back like hopping on a bicycle.

She decided it was time for bed. She flossed, brushed her teeth and took a quick rinse in the shower. She retrieved her cellphone from her recliner's armrest and went to her bedroom. She set her alarm clock at 6:00 a.m., hoping to make it to work before the interviewee.

She then remembered she hadn't even called him.

And that's when her train of thoughts started snowballing downhill. She had given her new boss one more reason to not like her. First, she had skipped him and directly communicated with the CEO for the financial

44

analyst selection process, when she should have known better. Then, she forgot to respond to a specific order. She could call tomorrow, but that wouldn't make her look any better in her director's eyes.

Then there was the whole idea of skipping five, potentially more qualified candidates, and call the eighth one on the list that she worked so hard to prepare when she once ran the HR all by herself. If her boss was pleased with her, the company's subsequent leaderships might not be. If they were pleased with her, the State of Michigan might not be. If she was legally fine, her conscience would still torment her for the rest of her life. Tom was obviously aware that Kirk's Brokerage was practically controlling Detroit's demographics, and he wanted to do his best to ensure that the company continued to "protect" Detroit and the northern suburbs from the immigrants across the railroad.

"I MISS YOU," said the text message that pinged from an unsaved number, which she recognized as belonging to a man she had met on a dating site months ago. Michelle had decided that it wasn't a good idea for her to have been on any dating website in the first place, let alone try multiple ones. There was a time when she felt too lonely. She had tried to meet her significant other, so she signed up for a free dating site. Her inbox was flooded with HI's, HEY's, and all kinds of pictures that had the exact reverse effect on her than what the senders had intended. She did end up reading a few profiles, respond to even fewer men, and go on a date with one of them. The man was nice at the time, but his later texts took another turn. She thought that the solution might be in signing up for a *paid* website. She ended up with another set of HI's and HEY's and pictures, and one other date.

"WE'RE NOT DOING THIS ANYMORE. I'D APPRECIATE IT IF YOU STOP TEXTING ME."

The next text was a sad face, followed by another text that was interrupted by a call from her mom.

"Hi, Shell."

"Mom, stop calling me Shell!" Michelle said with a chuckle.

A Railroad in Dearborn

"Did I wake you up, my girl?"

"No you're fine. How've you been?"

"I've signed up for the yoga class! I already made a new friend and we'll start on Monday!"

"I'm proud of you mom! I know you'll have so much fun."

"How are things with you? I just saw the news. Was that attack anywhere near you?"

"It's like ten minutes from where I work. I'm fine, mom. I guess. Life happens. I'll be alright."

"What happened, darling?"

"Nothing. It's just . . ." Michelle's voice was choked in her throat and she could feel it. Her eyes felt hot and her bedroom became blurry.

"Are you okay honey?"

"I am," Michelle said, wiping her eyes. "You remember how I wanted to work for Kirk's since I was young? I hope I didn't

47

make the wrong decision. This company has become something totally different. I mean, it's not the company, it's just the people here. It's so much different now that Kirk isn't running it."

"And where *is* Kirk?"

"No one knows, and that's the point. When he built the company, he wanted to serve the poor families and restore the city's economy so people could get jobs and live a better life. He did create a very successful company. Real-estate brokerage, loaning, investments, we do it all. It's just the wrong way now. The company now officially cares for the rich and not for the poor any longer. They want to segregate the whole city into a heaven and a hell, and the more time passes by, the more does it look like that's what we're doing."

"It's not your fault, honey. I believe in you. You just do what you think is right and it'll all be alright. You may need to find yourself another job. You can come back to Idaho whenever you want. I love you baby. Please let me know if you need anything. I'll always be there for you."

A Railroad in Dearborn

""Thanks mom, I know. I love you."

"I love you too Shell." Michelle gave a wet chuckle and hung up. She saw a text that read "FREE TOMORROW?" She blocked the number, deleted the text, and put her phone on silent. It didn't take her too long afterward to fall asleep.

X

"What's this? Where are we?" was the first intelligible thing Sadiq said to Falah, who was still on the wooden bench looking at him.

"I have no idea. Someone's basement," Falah said in Arabic.

Sadiq gave a blank stare at Falah that was both angry and scared. Falah realized that his new basement-mate didn't speak Arabic.

"We are kidnapped in a basement for old-style ransom money."

"Kidnapped? Who are they?"

"I think it's one very big dude who says he's Stanley."

Sadiq tried to spring up, before his motion was damped by his headache and vertigo. He slowed his movements, resting his head in his hand for a moment.

"*One* man?" Sadiq asked. "Who are you? How long have you been here? Oh man, it's midday and I already missed my interview!"

"Three days. You may want to save your energy. I've eaten one meal the whole time and it wasn't very good. I'm Falah, by the way."

"Sadiq. What happened? How did I end up here?"

"Stanley came carrying you like he was carrying a picnic mattress. I'd say the same way *I* ended up here. He was disguised as a police officer and pulled me over. I should've remembered that the police just don't come around here very often. The next thing I knew, I was on this bench, cellphone and wallet gone, and I was still bleeding."

"Is he armed?"

"I haven't seen any gun on him. He doesn't need one."

"You've been here for how long, locked up by one unarmed man and you didn't even *try* to free yourself? Dude you could've just surprised him with a punch on the nose! Look at all that junk around you,

you could've hit him on the head with a two-by-four!"

Before Falah could reply, the conversation was interrupted by Stanley's footsteps coming downstairs.

XI

"You people like your shish kabob, don't you? I brought you two wraps," announced Stanley, who was carrying a white plastic bag, as he entered the room.

Sadiq calmly walked toward Stanley, on his way to the door.

"Where are you going already, young man? Get back to where you've been."

"Try me," said Sadiq. Falah was watching with anticipation that soon turned into paralyzing horror.

"I said get back to . . ." by this time Stanley pushed Sadiq hard and threw him flat on his back to the floor.

Sadiq was so angry that he found enough energy to pick up a two-by-four and charge at Stanley, who threw the lunch bag on the floor. Sadiq swung the two-by-four aiming at Stanley's head. Stanley was calm, only raised his left hand and grabbed the board's end and pulled it out of Sadiq's hand. He threw it aside. All as quickly and easily as taking a toy bat from a child. Sadiq ran past

Stanley to the basement's door, but froze at the deafening sound of a bullet that whizzed right above his head, chipping the concrete wall above the door. Falah stayed frozen, shocked at open-fire in such an enclosed space.

"Get back. Now," Stanley growled at Sadiq.

The fear was obvious on Sadiq's face, who reluctantly raised his hands and walked backward.

"You would've been dead if I wanted you dead," Stanley said. "No need to raise your hands. Just sit on the floor where you were and don't make any stupid moves like that again." Sadiq obeyed.

"Atta boy," said Stanley. "Your families must be very proud of you both. You were going for your interview at Kirk's, weren't you?"

Sadiq looked up into Stanley's eyes with a look that showed hate, disgust, and fear.

A Railroad in Dearborn

"Answer me when I talk to you!" Stanley kicked Sadiq on his temple, and Sadiq screamed in pain.

"Yes! I was! What's wrong with you?"

"Everything, and nothing," Staley said. "I'm a man who loves his neighbors too much to let your little brains be poisoned by the deceptive mottos of a greedy real-estate firm. You don't know who these people are, you don't know what they're doing to you and to your community, but this will all change.

"I don't hate you. I love you and I want what's good for you. I appreciate your families' cooperation, so I promise you'll be back to them as soon as *they* decide. I haven't been successful in contacting your family. Whom should I call?"

At that point, a train sounded closer and closer. Falah and Sadiq both thought, for a split second, that they could not have been too far away from the railroad where they last saw the outdoors, maybe for the last time.

Stanley's eyes continued to focus on Sadiq's, though.

Sadiq was torn between speaking, thus getting his family involved in a situation that they were living too peaceful a life to cope with, and between not speaking and potentially having them lose him. Stanley shortened Sadiq's moment of hesitation when Stanley narrowed his eyes at him.

"Layla."

"Thank you," Stanley replied. He picked up the white food bag, took two aluminum-foil wraps and threw each one to each of his two hostages, both of whom missed them. He walked out afterwards and locked the door. The two boys were much calmer by now and became even calmer as Stanley's retreating footsteps became silent.

"He has a gun," Falah said.

"Shut up."

A Railroad in Dearborn

XII

"What time will your class end?" Asked Louis after he dropped Aziz off at the Dearborn English School. He had finally been pushed to the point of taking his coworker to learn English. Up until now, Aziz hadn't really needed to know much English to work at the packaging department of the auto-industry logistics company where they both worked, which he didn't even know its title.

"Time? Pick-up?" Louis had to motion to Aziz, who was dumbfounded by a strange accent of a language he wished he was more familiar with. Eventually, Louis pointed to his watch.

"Don't know," replied Aziz. "One. First," showing his right hand's index finger.

"One o'clock? You're not staying here until after midnight, are you?"

Aziz's face was frozen. His eyes spoke of confusion and embarrassment.

"Oh!" Louis figured out. "This is your *first* class! Let me speak to your teacher." Louis turned off his car and walked into the school. Although Louis had worked with Arabs for a decade, this was the first time he saw that many head covers in one place, and that confused him for a minute, before he thought how ridiculous it was to be scared by the Arab women when he practically knew every Arab man he saw at Walmart.

"Excuse me, ma'am!" Women turned and walked away. A few of them looked at him but they looked like deer in headlights.

"Uh . . . Ma'am, 'scuse me," Louis made a few whistles, hoping that one of them would land at anyone who knew any English. Finally, one woman walked out of what looked like a classroom.

"Sir, this is the women's door."

"Oh, I'm sorry! I didn't know that."

"It's okay. How can I help you?

"Uh . . . my friend here wants to learn English. Where should he go?" That's when Louis realized that Aziz hadn't entered into the building with him. "He must still be outside, and now I know why."

"The door in the back. Does he have his driver's license or any photo I.D.?"

"I think so. Thanks ma'am, and sorry! What time should I pick him up?"

"Class ends at 7:00 p.m."

Louis nodded, gave the thumbs-up and walked outside, while Layla walked back to her classroom. She automatically pulled her phone from her pocket and checked it.

A missed call and a voice message from Sadiq.

Layla wanted to check the voice message, but then decided that her brother could wait. He may have wanted to tell her that he got the job.

Layla began her class on time, and the phone was never checked again until late that evening, when Layla went to bed around midnight.

XIII

"We can't be locked up here forever. I can't *believe* no one knows about us yet. Did *no* one see either of us kidnapped in broad daylight in a major city? Didn't those at Kirk's miss us? Did no one see either of our cars? This is not happening! If this is happening to us then it can happen to anyone anywhere at any time!"

"*My* family knows," Falah said, "and I think they promised to pay the ransom money and not call the police, and hence the shish-kabob. Stanley told me he called them and said they were cooperative. Forget Kirk's. *Everyone* wants to work there. They will hardly ever remember that we had job interview appointments."

"I don't feel optimistic about this at all," said Sadiq, walking toward the basement door as if to check out something.

"Look at that!" Sadiq picked up the casing of the bullet that nearly hit him and started investigating it. "It's a .45 Glock!"

"Huh?"

A Railroad in Dearborn

"This bullet can kill a horse! Two horses standing next to each other!"

"Now you're making that up."

"No, seriously! This man isn't playing games. He's either a veteran or a Militia, or both." Falah looked at Sadiq, waiting for him to explain terms totally unfamiliar to him.

"Detroit Militia? Haven't you heard of them?" Sadiq asked.

"God help us. No, I have not."

"It's an anti-government militia that's been there since the early 1990s.

"White supremacists?"

"No, they have whites and blacks and all. I don't know, Stanley doesn't look like a professional fighter. Most of them are veterans. I'm sure he isn't. But this gun . . . this man means business!"

"Anti-government? Then why does he sound mad at Kirk's?"

"I don't know," Sadiq replied. "Kirk's is practically doing them a favor, serving the locals like him across the railroad at our own expense—unless he lives in Dearborn too."

"Kirk's works for *all* the Detroit area. My family got a loan from them and we were able to build our house when the company first started. They relieved us from almost half of the loan. I could not have finished school had my family not owned our house."

"So *you* say. Kirk was an evil genius who wanted to segregate Detroit into the rich and the poor. Your loan was a smoke screen to cover up his anti-immigrant sentiments."

"Did you say *was*?"

"He died long ago."

"How do you know? I tried to look him up but I didn't see any trace of him. They said he's discreetly building similar companies everywhere and serving many communities. I've always been obsessed with him. Why would he do that? How can he make any profit? How could he accomplish

62

so much and still stays under the radar so much that he doesn't even have a Wikipedia article on him?"

"You've been brainwashed," said Sadiq. "That's what he *wanted* you to think. I don't know if you notice it or not, but not a single Arab household that I know of has qualified for a grant or even a loan from the company in a long time. They have so many projects—*all* of which are in Detroit and the northern suburbs. Our community has declined so much not even the government could restore the law and order in this place anymore. Look at us, we'll stay in a stinky basement forever if we live to see it and no one will know."

"You said you were on your way to Kirk's."

"I was. They pay well and I wanted to give it a shot. I knew I should not have gone."

Falah and Sadiq had so much in common, they realized, and so many differences, but not enough energy to keep talking. They were both in their early twenties. Both Arabs. Both studied finance (though in two different universities). Falah thought that Sadiq was too much of a negative energy to listen to, so he ignored the rest of his complaints and allowed himself to lie back on the wooden bench and fall asleep.

A Railroad in Dearborn

XIV

"Mom!" Screamed Layla, as she ran from her bedroom to the living room. "Mom! Sadiq has been kidnapped!"

"Have you lost your mind, girl? What are you talking about?"

"Sadiq is kidnapped! Oh God! I didn't see my phone until now! Listen to this!"

Layla played a voice message and turned the speaker on. Stanley's voice was so calm it was chilling:

"Hi. I have your son, er . . . Sadiq (Sadeeq?) I have him with me. He is safe and sound and is well taken care of. You have until next Wednesday to come up with fifty thousand dollars in cash to have him back as good as when you last saw him. Call me when you have the money. I would recommend that you don't call the police and be as discreet as you can. Hope to see you next week."

Um Sadiq broke into a calm prayer, and then silence. She closed her eyes and teared up.

"Where can we come up with this much money?" Layla said. "Sadiq is gone! I *told* him not to go to Detroit in the early morning! Your son would just not listen to sound advice!"

Um Sadiq gently blew her nose. "Can't we apply for a loan?"

"What loan? Are you crazy? What bank would approve a loan this fast? A week won't be enough to do anything! Loan, equity, wiring money from Uncle Khalid in Baghdad or anything!"

"I'll have to call Sheikh Husham. I hope the mosque can come up with the money. Call the Sheikh."

"It's already after midnight, mom!"

"Just call him, will you." Layla would have argued calling anyone that late in normal circumstances. She searched her phone's contacts and pressed *Sheikh*. The phone rang four times, then the call was answered.

"Um Sadiq?"

"Hello, Sheikh. Sorry to wake you up. Here's my mom," Layla gave the phone to her mom, who was still maintaining her composure, even though her eyes were red from crying.

"Hello, Sheikh"

"What's up, Um Sadiq?"

"Sadiq has . . ." at that point, Um Sadiq's voice failed her. There was silence, followed by a monotonic, high-pitched noise, then another silence.

"Um Sadiq, are you okay? What's going on?"

"Sadiq has been kidnapped! My little son!" She let go of her sobs. "He went out this morning for a job interview and didn't come back, and now a man called us and said he would release him for fifty thousand!" Layla listened to her mom, and heard the Sheikh's unintelligible voice.

"From *his* phone."

Pause.

"Sadiq's phone, yes."

Pause.

"I don't know! Where can I *possibly* come up with all that money?"

Another pause.

"I'll let Layla drive me," She turned to her daughter, "Are you going to the pharmacy tomorrow?"

"Forget work, mom, what did he say?"

"Thank you, Sheikh. God bless." Um Sadiq gave the phone back to Layla, who pressed the red button.

"The Sheikh said that I need to go and see him tomorrow at eight."

Layla calculated her schedule for the next day. The anxiety of the night was paralyzing: there was no way she could contact her workplace to say she would be late for work at that time. She was suddenly interested in knowing where her brother was, even though he would stay out for days some times without telling her. She was resisting the urge, though with difficulty, to call his kidnapper. Even if the Sheikh did come up with that much money that fast, it may become a liability of some kind for a long time, and it wouldn't guarantee bringing Sadiq back safely. Could anyone trust a kidnapper? What if he took the money and *didn't* return Sadiq? Would it be a good idea to call the police instead?

Layla stayed with her mom for another hour without saying a word. They both stared at the TV, not paying any attention to the Syrian soap opera. She eventually became too tired and went back to her room, but she wouldn't sleep for another hour. She was looking at her phone against her habit, and she replayed Stanley's voice message over and over again. The night felt like a sleepless night.

XV

"Did you hear about Steve Kidds?" Said Travis, sipping his morning coffee at Michelle's cubicle.

"Yeah. I've heard that he flopped his interview."

"Man, Tom must feel ridiculous now! I can't believe how he expects to do HR in his first week at work. This man has never done that in the past. He has no idea what the protocols are and he sure looks bold enough to override the system!"

"Kirk's system will *not* be overridden," Michelle said. "This is not what I signed up for. Our company employs the best from everywhere and serves everybody. Sooner or later, Tom will have to do things right or the company will go down. The same goes for Paul. We are not just any company and I'm pretty sure we would not have been able to sustain ourselves all that time without Kirk."

"That's what I'm afraid of, Michelle," Travis said. "Kirk isn't around anymore and he might as well be dead.

A Railroad in Dearborn

People are not seeing us as philanthropists any more. Just another greedy real-estate and loaning company, and we're not even doing it right. Detroit isn't any less of a challenge than when the company first started. There's still so much work that needs to be done, and the economy doesn't look promising enough for us to stand on our own. I don't know . . . I think we need to start shopping for a more secure job before we get the pink slip."

"Yeah," said Michelle, as she stood to head toward the staff kitchen to get her lunch wrap and Coke. She had been feeling down the past few days, and she refused to let Travis make her day any worse. On the one hand, his concern was totally legitimate: the protocol that Kirk had put for the company had been reinterpreted in the past two decades. It was supposed to work for the good of the whole Detroit metro area, but now it seemed the company was only working for downtown Detroit, in addition to the richer suburbs in the north. It was supposed to be an equal opportunity employer, but now that equal opportunity was only available for a specific demographic. The recent terror attacks had only justified that policy, and that sure didn't help. Kirk's was not prepared to be a standalone investments company. Its assignment was extremely larger than its resources, and it was underemployed. It would need a long time for the newer employees to be trained enough to carry the weight of Detroit on their shoulders, and even longer if they did not have the basic competence in the first place.

Michelle shook her head dry as she walked back to her cubicle. This company was not going down on her watch. She was absolutely invested in her work to serve the community and she knew that Kirk was coming back. He might even be following up with his company from somewhere else. Her pride was taking her all the way through whatever would happen to the company and she knew she would survive the current crisis. She may even be promoted at Kirk's return. After all, that's how great people are made: when they successfully pass such a fiery furnace. To quit now would land her in a lower job, if any, where she would have to restart her career from scratch. Even worse, if her company sprang back to how it used to be in its heyday, she would not forgive herself for the rest of her life for not being there to see it.

Travis had already returned to his cubicle. The break was officially over. Michelle sat at her desk and stared at her computer monitor. She moved her mouse and the screensaver disappeared and uncovered an email alert that read "Steve's Employment Letter."

"Oh boy," Michelle sighed.

XVI

By his fourth day as a hostage, Falah was becoming adapted to Stanley's basement and, much to his horror, was feeling more hopeful. He knew that this situation would end either in his release or death—although death was the most likely, considering that he hasn't eaten enough and he was in neither the physical shape nor the mood to earn his freedom through Stanley. His new basement-mate may have helped him feel a little better had he not been a dark conspiracy theorist, sharing the same rhetoric of his own kidnapper. It was very odd that Sadiq, the Arab young man who was kidnapped when he was on his way to a job interview at Kirk's, agreed with Stanley that the company was the reason behind Dearborn's misery. Why would Stanley care about Dearborn, Sadiq did not bother to question.

The sound of the approaching train muffled Stanley's footsteps as he was coming downstairs. Falah's fear of being adapted to his hostage situation was just confirmed, when he knew that his next meal was, finally, on the way.

A Railroad in Dearborn

"You two are doing alright down there?" asked Stanley, before the basement door was open enough for him to get inside. Sadiq was too somber for the sound of the plastic bag of food to cheer him up.

"Falafel anyone?" Stanley threw the plastic bag to Sadiq, as if he was the most favorite, after their unmatched fight the day before.

Sadiq's look, in turn, wasn't friendly, and he didn't bother to catch what might have been the only meal for the day, or the last meal.

"Keep it up!" sneered Stanley, as he turned to leave.

"What do you want?" Falah was impressed with Sadiq's bold tone.

Stanley looked back at Sadiq so fast like he did not want to miss a once-in-a-lifetime scene. He looked like he'd been waiting for someone to oppose, or even to resist him. He showed a smile of satisfaction, but his eyes weren't prepared for the answer to that basic question.

"What do *I* want? It's not what I want, my friend, it's what *everyone* wants. Look at you! You're history in the making, man! You have been wronged all along and no one would listen to you or your family! You were neglected, and now those cowards across the railroad will start recognizing you! Your community will have its due dignity, your people will be respected as they should have always been, and all you have to do is to enjoy your free food and housing until the Day of the Poor comes!"

"You're kidnapping us out of your love for Arabs?"

"Why don't you look at it as . . ." Stanley looked aside, thinking of a good illustration, like he was talking with a business partner. "A means to an end. Low collateral damage for a greater good. A temporary, inconvenient situation for a permanent solution. This is not the way kidnapping works. You have neither been assaulted, nor your dignity insulted. Your belongings are safe upstairs and it won't be too long before you leave."

A Railroad in Dearborn

"You have kidnapped us for ransom money," Sadiq retorted. "This trick isn't even good enough to be called the oldest in the book. Why us? What's with you and Kirk's?"

Falah closed his eyes for a second, like he didn't want to see the inevitable result of his friend's sudden, unnecessary boldness.

"Let me tell you this story . . ." Stanley said, like he'd been waiting for this time to open up.

"My family used to have a farm. Very large farm right here near Mount Pleasant," Stanley showed his open palm to Sadiq and pointed to the middle of it. "Five hundred acres. My father used to run that farm, and he inherited it from his father. It was our family's main business. We had cattle and all and we grew everything. So many people were making a living working for our farm.

"Then in the late nineties, guess what? Kirk's comes out of nowhere, with a diabolical government scheme to allegedly 'help the poor in the inner cities.' To cover up his government funding, he was buying properties everywhere to flip them. He started with the larger properties outside of Detroit, those who could generate more money faster for him.

"My father refused to sell his farm. Those fools, believing that Kirk was a divine savior, quit working at our farm. We lost too much money to sustain our business in one season. My father ended up taking his own life.

"Kirk practically used a family's heritage, our own legacy, to execute a foolish master plan in a city that has been doomed with bankruptcy, riddled with crime, addiction and filth. That's when we decided to take matters into our own hands to restore our community from those socialists, so don't tell me I have no right in having a personal feud with Kirk's."

"You are the sickest man I've ever met."

"A sick man with *your* money, whose cause will be vindicated," Stanley said with a warm smile.

78

A Railroad in Dearborn

"Us. It's about us," Sadiq said. "Your father's property and death wouldn't have brought you all the way to live in Dearborn if it wasn't that you hated us more than you loved your father."

"Just hope your family will call me back by Wednesday, young man," Stanley said as he calmly turned around, left the basement and locked the door.

"Across the railroad."

"Across the railroad." said both Falah and Sadiq at the same time. "We're not too far away from Greenfield and Warren."

"And you're right. He's a Detroit Militia."

XVII

"ALL DEPARTMENTS, STAFF MEETING," said the text on Skype. Michelle saved her Excel sheet before she closed it and looked from above her cubicle partition to see Travis's face, who looked back at her in turn. They both gave each other the same dissatisfied, sarcastic look.

Travis walked out first and Michelle followed. They were joined by a dozen employees from the other departments walking all the way to Paul's office. That helped soothe the usually tense atmosphere associated with surprise meetings with the CEO.

"I would like first to express how impressed I am with the excellent performance of our staff," started Paul Canty, knowing that every employee was waiting for bad news. "For the past two decades," he continued, "and especially since Kirk handed over our company's leadership to its first CEO after him, you have been assigned a historic work. Our city was ill-reputed, and now many major companies are moving back in. The automobile industry is thriving once again and people who once were unable to pay their bills have received loans and grants that have helped our city look all the more beautiful. You have been on the frontline of this task.

"With the ever-expanding work that we have, with the acquiring of the old Train Station, and with the dwindling resources that you know we have, we've been trying to delicately balance between our staff and our work. The more employees we hire, the more resources we will need that we may not have. Still, if we do not increase our staff, we won't be able to keep up with the work."

Michelle's eyebrows rose as she looked at the impressed Travis, sitting next to her.

"I believe in our company," Paul continued, looking at each of them in turn, "and I think we need to hire more employees. We have made it in the last two decades very well, and we can continue our performance well into the future, even if we had to go through a few hiccups. I will ask for more new staff members to be trained by you. You should not be working all by yourselves. What do you think?"

No one answered.

Michelle noticed that Tom was sitting next to Paul. She assumed that the HR had already shared its department's thoughts.

"Michelle?" asked Paul, almost startling her.

"I . . . uh . . . I think this is a great idea," Michelle began. "I know that Tom knows what's best for the company and I trust his vision regarding the HR role in this process." Tom showed neither approval nor disapproval in Michelle's little lie.

"Very good," Paul replied. "Until you get someone to help you, you will be in charge of the employment process. Tom said he trusts your experience in this area. We want your department to work as a team. IT?"

The meeting continued through with the IT, finance, compliance, contracts and other departments, all of which showed, in turn, puzzled appreciation for the plan to hire

82

new team members without defining the financial part. More employees should make more money for the company, they all hoped, but that required Kirk's Brokerage to perform somewhere near perfect.

The employees were served cake and Cokes, and they had cordial conversations amongst themselves, before they were dismissed to their departments.

As Michelle was accompanying Travis back to their office, she heard Tom's voice from behind her saying "Michelle," and she turned around.

"Would you be in my office in five minutes?"

"Sure."

Tom was sitting behind his desk when Michelle came into his office.

"You little liar, you!" said Tom with a smile.

"I seriously meant it," Michelle smiled back. "I mean, that's why you're the director, isn't it?"

"Yeah, yeah, yeah," thanks to Paul's meeting, Michelle felt comfortable in Tom's office for the first time since he became her boss.

"Michelle. I have said it before and I'll say it again. Your reputation is going before you. You have a good report and you've built a name for yourself in this company in the few years you've been working here. I want your honesty to, let's just say, walk hand-in-hand with your wisdom.

"You will be in charge of hiring people. Whatever you do will affect our community. You may not realize it but you have the most important job in Detroit. In this whole nation. In the world."

Tom may not be exaggerating, Michelle thought. Kirk's has been in charge of reviving a world-class metropolis, one of the biggest in the world and, apart from the segregational side effect which was not originally planned, is still reputed to be a benevolent firm to those it served.

"I want you to be in charge of both the advertisement and the selection

84

processes. I know you'll do a good job in studying the prospective employees' profiles, and I want you to interview them."

"Me?"

"I'll be out of town for a week. Paul is kind of in a hurry. I'll lobby a few investors in Wall Street for the next stage of our company."

"You want me to advertise, study profiles, interview and employ in a *week*?"

"Whoa, slow down, you won't *employ* anyone. That's why Paul and I are here. You will only *recommend*."

"That's what I meant."

"Then yes. It won't take too long for the *Free P.* to put the advertisement. Let's try *Indeed* too this time."

"Okay," Michelle said. "I just wanted you to know that I have the protocols and the laws to work according to. You know that I cannot go against our protocols or the State of Michigan, you know that people will be applying from everywhere the moment they see the advertisement. I understand your concerns, but I cannot go against my career and my conscience when the one with the perfect profile applies."

"What do you mean?"

"Sir, you know what I mean. Most of those who apply are U of M graduates, most of whom happen to live across the railroad."

"Okay?"

"So, if while you're on your trip, I happen to recommend one of them, will you be . . ," Michelle stalled, surprised to see that Tom wasn't protesting her argument. He looked like they had never had any similar conversation earlier that week.

"Not at all. Why would I? Kirk's is an equal-opportunity employer. I just wanted you to know that whoever you employ may be influential enough to lead the company, perhaps our whole community, one way or another."

"That's why I'd love for the process to be done under your direct supervision."

A Railroad in Dearborn

"Michelle . . . you'll be fine. Just choose the best for our company and for Detroit according to your training and instinct."

Michelle nodded.

"And your conscience," Tom added.

Apparently, the two had different definitions of the word "conscience."

XVIII

"Don't die on me, young man, you'll walk home in any minute now. Or any day. Hopefully," said Stanley to a feeble Falah, who started to look scrawny on his fifth day in the basement. Falah's passive demeanor might have been what was keeping him alive thus far. He reserved his energy by lying on the bench most of the time, only talking when necessary, and he would've been in a better mood had his only company not been constantly talking about the world after the Apocalypse. Still, Falah was encouraged by Sadiq's robust look. *Sadiq isn't dead yet, neither would I be for a while*, Falah thought.

"If you think I'm buying your food and hosting you here for free forever, you're wrong. You're lucky your family loves you. I hope they'll keep their promise." He threw a slider wrapped in wax fast-food paper toward Falah.

"And you, buddy," Stanley addressed Sadiq, "I hope Layla or whatever her name is has received my voice mail." He threw the other slider to Sadiq, walked out and locked the basement door.

A Railroad in Dearborn

"Has anyone not seen our cars anywhere?" Sadiq asked, to no one in particular. "Did no business on Warren have any cameras? Can people just get police uniforms and walk around completely unsuspected?"

"We've been through that, Sadiq."

"The problem is," Falah rolled his eyes and tried to regain his appetite for his only meal for the day. Fortunately for him, Sadiq wasn't expecting his attention as he went on ranting. "We happen to live on the wrong side of the railroad. The problem isn't who we are as people, it's just where we were doomed to be born. I don't think Stanley is a career criminal. We may pretty much be his only victims. I mean look at him: why would he bother feeding us? He may know that we could survive for more than a week without food, and he said that we're only staying here for a week."

"After which . . ." Falah gestured for Sadiq to keep going.

"Look, I don't think he's gonna kill us or something. He's bluffing for money, old school, and that's it. He thinks all Arabs are rich and he just wants to blackmail us. Stanley isn't responsible for the situation here in Dearborn. Just think about it: you would've done the same thing had you lost your way of life to a different people. I mean he lost his farm, his father . . ."

"Dude, farmers don't kill themselves after one loss in one season. There's much more to the story than what he said."

"Still," Sadiq said, as if that alone was an argument.

Falah was now more concerned with the sudden change of attitude in his partner than the twenty pounds he had lost in the past few days. "Stanley is a man with a cause," continued Sadiq, "and we happened to be on his way, and not even for long. He's a patriot who loves his people. He's dedicated and well-organized.

"Kirk, on the other hand," Sadiq went on. Falah struggled to chew his slider, "Kirk is the real problem. At least Stanley didn't pretend to care about us. Kirk made a whole business in the name of benevolence and equality, only to disintegrate the Arab

90

community in Dearborn. He spoke of love and we believed him. He forgave a few loans here and there and people blindly bought into his scheme."

Falah resisted the urge to ask Sadiq why did he apply to work for Kirk's, but decided to save himself from another potentially endless discourse.

"And you know what," Sadiq wasn't finished, "you may be right. Kirk might very well be alive. Someone needs to fund and run an unusual business like his firm. Kirk's poses as a company, but it can't be more than one man's business. A really rich man who has managed to stay under the radar the whole time."

Sadiq's speech was interrupted by the sound of an approaching train, and that's when he realized he didn't have any conclusion to his homily, and he reluctantly started eating his bland slider.

XIX

Michelle had two reasons not to interrupt her boss's trip on its first day with a phone call. First, she didn't want that to be done to her either. She remembered her Ludington vacation from last year, when she was literally in her swimsuit in Lake Michigan, trying to take a selfie, when her former boss texted her "WHERE IS THE ARENA'S CONTRACT?" which ruined the rest of her day.

The second, bigger reason was that she knew Tom wouldn't like to see the list of the applicants for the various positions in the company. As she expected, most of them happened to be from the southern suburbs, and their profiles were very impressive. On one hand, she wanted to be comforted by the thought of Tom reminding her that she was fully in charge of the process. Nevertheless, she thought she knew Tom well enough to not trust his reaction when he knew who was being employed at Kirk's. At one point, the new staff would be in control so much they could launch the company's projects in their own hometowns, Dearborn or Melvindale or Taylor. They would benefit their people, maybe at the expense of those being benefitted now. They could even move their families across the railroad. They would redistribute the Detroit population, in Tom's mind, and be responsible for another Detroit decline that the company had been working to reverse for two decades.

Michelle prepared and sent an official email, attaching the list of the applicants with the proper profiles to the relevant executives, and had Travis print out the interview appointment letters for the rest of that Monday.

"Should be special," said Travis as he was struggling to spell the applicants names. "I mean, don't get me wrong, I'm looking forward to working with them. I just don't know how long will it be before Tom loses his mind when he see the new faces though."

"Honestly," Michelle said, "I've been thinking the same the whole weekend. I wish I could say it doesn't bother me, but it does. I've been waiting to see this moment in the company for a long time. It's like its old days. It'll look so beautiful when it's more diverse, when there is a real intention of serving the needy around us instead of making the rich richer and the poor poorer. I didn't think of the tension we'll have to deal with until the newer employees are trained and well-established. One mistake and it'll be my fault. Maybe not even a mistake. One story in the news from the Middle East and it'll all be my fault." Travis chuckled at Michelle's joke.

Her computer sounded a new email alert. It was from Tom who, naturally, was one of the recipients of her earlier email.

"Here we go," said Michelle with a smile, as she opened the email.

Tom was questioning all the basic procedures he should have known Michelle had already gone through. He especially emphasized the security background checks, and asked about their legal status. He didn't leave their educational records unquestioned either.

Michelle replied quickly that she covered all that. A few seconds later, her phone rang.

A Railroad in Dearborn

"Hi Tom . . ." Michelle answered.

"I did," Michelle said.

A long pause. Travis raised his eyebrows.

"I know. That's what I said," Michelle said. There was a long pause, during which Michelle's smile slowly disappeared. Travis was watching with anticipation.

"I can wait until you come back.

"Okay . . . Thanks sir. Bye." Michelle hung up.

"What did he say?"

"Nothing. Interviews first thing in the morning tomorrow as planned."

XX

Nora was so overwhelmed with her seventh workday at Al-Yasmeen that she started to think it might not have been a good idea to work in a Middle-Eastern restaurant. She had been looking for a job to support herself and her mother after recent move from Albania. Although fast-food places always looked for more people to hire, the hope of making more money being tipped by those Arab spenders when they see pretty girls attracted her to that restaurant. The food wasn't that authentic, she thought, so it shouldn't be crowded. Now she started to realize that the place was popular among both locals and immigrants.

She had just picked up the last plate from a table that had a party of eight, and decided to pick up the silverware and the napkins in another trip, when she eyed a man parking his Chevy in the parking lot through the window. The vehicle was too wide for a 1990s model, but it was in a good shape. The man, well in his sixties, with white hair, polo shirt and old jeans, didn't look rich enough to be a good tipper either, but what did Nora know about people. And besides, she had already been making a decent living in this short amount of time.

The place was already crowded for lunch time, so she knew that she would be the one who served him. There wasn't any available place other than the large table she was cleaning. She ran to the kitchen, impressed with herself for carrying that many plates, placed them by the sink, picked the table-cleaning spray, a rag and a plastic box, and ran back to the table. She threw everything that was on the table in the box, and sprayed and wiped the table clean as the man entered.

The man was tall and had a grandfatherly demeanor that was easy to notice. He had a personable smile. His jeans weren't pressed, and he needed to straighten out his polo shirt's collar and maybe shine his boots or at least wipe the dust off them. Everything about him was old, except his eyes.

"I'll be right back with you, sir!" said Nora. In a split-second, she could feel that he was more like a family member she had known for years than a customer she had just seen. She decided to serve this old grandpa well regardless of his tip.

The man helped himself to a seat near the far end of the table, when he saw the free copies of the Arab newspapers on a small table by the window. He walked there out of curiosity, which was increased when he saw that one paper was in two languages. He picked a copy and looked at it and, at that moment, the nearby railroad crossing's signal sounded off. He calmly looked at the approaching train emerging from the south like he was reminiscing over the sight of an old friend. He stood where he was and shifted his sight to the Hollingsworth building across the street, which looked as old as when he last saw it, until the train passed the crossing. He turned back and went toward his seat.

"My name is Nora," she introduced herself, bringing a clean napkin and silverware to him. The old man lifted his eyes off the newspaper to give his server an I-know look that almost intimidated her, "and I'll be your server for today. Can I start you off with something to drink?"

A Railroad in Dearborn

"Hi Nora," the man's voice was as deep as life. He was so charismatic he sounded like he meant every word he said. He almost sounded like he was teaching his server her own name, "Coffee, please. Black."

Nora automatically looked as his hands and, as perfect as it would have been in another universe, there was no ring on any of his fingers.

"You have a beautiful smile, Nora," the old man said, at which time Nora lost it and hoped her goofy smile hadn't bailed on her every thought.

"Thank you! The menu is on the table." Normally, Nora would leave immediately, but she was caught in the anticipation of another flattering word from Mr. Charming.

"I think I'll go ahead and order," said the man without lifting his eyes off Nora's. She couldn't tell whether the man was smiling or just the way he normally looked. "The place doesn't look much different from what it looked like when I had my last dinner here years ago."

"I have only been working here for a week. I hope it doesn't look too bad," said Nora with a giggle.

"Not at all, I love it! It may not be Red Lobster, but I love the food here."

"We had a few Middle-Eastern restaurants in Albania, where I come from, but I still can't tell if the food here is authentic or not." He was looking at her with a monotonic attention, as if he was not surprised by anything she was saying. "The management here is good, though, and everyone says they like it."

"I'm sure some of them like it because of you. I'm Gilbert, by the way.

"Kirk Gilbert."

A Railroad in Dearborn

XXI

It took Stanley the best part of a minute to know which of the two cellphones, plugged next to each other, belonged to which of his kidnappees.

"Do you have the money?"

"Let me talk to my brother."

"You're not the one making the rules here, ma'am. Do you have the cash?"

"You won't get anything before I hear Sadiq's voice, you punk. Now let me hear his voice."

"Sadiq is fine. You'll have him back the moment I get the money. Don't you trust me?"

"I don't trust *anyone*. Let me talk to Sadiq for a minute, and I'll tell you how to get the money."

"No, no, no, you don't understand the game, sweetheart. *You* get the money ready, and *I'll* tell you when and where should we meet," Stanley said as he picked up the keys from the coffee table and started downstairs.

Both Falah and Sadiq were lying almost motionless, exactly where he had last left them. They gave him empty stares once they saw him, and not one of them made a move.

"This is for you, handsome man," Stanley whispered as he covered the phone's bottom with his hand. "Don't make any smart moves and be careful what you say. Okay?"

Sadiq's eyes opened wide with surprise, while Falah's face shone with the long-awaited hope.

"Hello?" Sadiq didn't know that his voice has become softer, more tired, but his sister certainly realized the difference.

Both Stanley and Falah watched Sadiq with an impatient anticipation. When he closed his eyes and started tearing up, Stanley's impatience increased, while Falah's turned into a sadness that was long-due to be realized.

A Railroad in Dearborn

"How's mom?" Was the only thing he managed to say, before Stanley snatched the phone back from him.

"You believe me now, sweetheart? If this is a game you're playing, your dear brother won't live to see tonight." Stanley walked out of the basement and locked the door. The last thing the two boys heard was a fading "I'll call you tomorrow in the morning to let you know . . ."

There was a long silence, interrupted by a few, suppressed sobs.

"I hope they're careful," said Falah.

"So do I," Sadiq said after a snuffle. "She said they'll get me real soon and she sounded confident. I think the mosque came up with the ransom money. There's no other way they could've . . ." Both Sadiq and Falah looked at each other as they both sped up to the same conclusion.

"The phone! Is our man really that stupid?"

XXII

"How do you pronounce your name?"

"Ahmed Farhan. Farhan is Arabic for 'happy.'"

"Oh, I've heard this name a lot but I didn't know that!" Michelle felt she had the easiest and the most fun job that day. Kirk's Brokerage was interviewing its future employees, and the waiting room was barely spacious enough to accommodate all those who were invited that morning. The security officers were showing an unusual presence, and the staff were already seeing that it would not be a day for them to socialize and gossip.

"So, it says here that you've become a U.S. citizen in the year 2000?"

Ahmed's face turned from attentive to friendly.

Then from friendly to panicked, over what sounded like an explosion.

"Oh my God! What was that?" screamed Travis.

104

A Railroad in Dearborn

The explosion could not have been a blown tire—not at the thirty-third floor of the RenCen. It could not have an electric failure with the powerful gust that shattered the main office room's north window. If it wasn't caused by a faulty a gas pipe, then it was the worst news imaginable on every level.

"Oh God! What is what?" was mixed with a louder, thicker voice that said "Get down and stay down!" from what sounded like a security officer.

Both Michelle and Ahmed were under the same desk now, practically hugging each other and not even knowing it. Their faces showed blank stares as they waited to know what had happened, or whether or not the worst was over.

"Okay everyone get from underneath the tables and let's get out of here. Now! C'mon let's move!" By the time the employees and the interviewee came out of their hiding place, the way to the staircase was lined with security officers showing the way and urging to move. The waiting room had a few blood stains on the floor and on a few seats. The place was filled with dust and shattered glass.

The employees met with paramedics running opposite them, supposedly to respond to what they would remember later as injured people laid against the western wall of the waiting room. No one could tell who was injured and who, if any, was dead.

After three flights of stairs, the employees were systematically led to the express elevators going all the way down to the first floor. It was when the elevator's door was shut that Michelle remembered that she was carrying her phone all along. The phone was on silent, and when she checked it, she saw a ton of text messages and missed calls, from her mom, from Tom, and an unknown New York number.

A Railroad in Dearborn

XXIII

"What was that?" Stanley interrupted his own list of instructions when he heard a boom coming from the north, but Layla did not answer.

"You people are crazy. You're *all* crazy and you don't deserve to live!" Stanley shouted into the phone.

"Yeah, the world would be much better if everyone in it was like you," Layla's voice was too blank to sound sarcastic. Still, Stanley struggled to hear her as he was standing in the parking lot of a baklava place that was already getting crowded.

"Shut up and listen," Stanley said, fighting his panic and frustration at the boom and at this rude woman. "On Thursday at 6 p.m., that's two days from now in the afternoon, you will come to the Roosevelt Park, opposite the old Train Station, park your car there and wait for my instructions. I will be watching you from everywhere. If I see anyone else with you, your brother dies. I hope I'm making myself clear on this.

"You will have fifty thousand dollars with you in used, non-sequential bills in different denominations. The money needs to be in a sports duffle bag.

"I will need to know the make of your car and what your duffle bag looks like."

There was no answer.

"Do we have any problem here?" Stanley asked.

"2004 grey Taurus. U of M blue bag."

"Good girl.

"What the . . ." Stanley's call was interrupted by the unexpected view of Sadiq running out of Chase Road.

He calmly put his phone in his pocket and started walking toward Warren and Chase, slowly then faster. By the time he arrived at the intersection, he stood for a moment, hesitated between following his kidnappee in public, and between going to his house and see what was going on and figuring out how he managed to escape. Did
108

he get any help from anyone? Was the other kidnappee there? How much time did he have before his place was discovered?

By the time the panicked Stanley arrived at his house, he saw the Altima still parked in front of it. The house's front door was shut, so he used his keys to open it and get inside the house that looked exactly as messy as when he had left it minutes ago, even the two cellphones were still being charged next to each other. He ran downstairs and saw that the basement door was wide open.

The lockset was on the floor, along with a screwdriver and a few screws.

And a scrawny Falah was peacefully sleeping on his wooden bench.

XXIV

"I'm fine. I guess everyone is fine. The explosion happened either in the reception room or just outside it," Michelle's voice was still shaking as she spoke to Tom through her handsfree car phone. Tom was already at the airport, waiting on a standby list for the next flight to Detroit.

"I'm watching the news at the airport now and it says that two are already confirmed dead and the death toll is expected to rise. Are you sure you've checked on all our people? I couldn't get hold of anyone else."

"Sir, I saw the . . ." Michelle's voice was lost in a sob followed by a snuffle, then she tried again in a higher pitch, "I saw the dead and the injured. They're all from among the interviewees." Her voice returned to near-normal, "We were all led simultaneously out of the building and I'm sure we're all accounted for."

"Good. Michelle, we have been talking about that for a while now, and I won't be polite anymore when there are lives in danger."

110

A Railroad in Dearborn

Michelle's fear and sadness suddenly turned into disgust at Tom's words. "We will start doing major changes in our policies. Over my dead body will those across the railroad get the city. No more applications from the southern suburbs, am I clear on this?"

"I just told you that all the victims were from across the railroad, you moron!" Michelle let an unchecked burst of anger take her dumbfounded manager by a pleasant surprise.

"Did you just call me a moron?"

Michelle hung up.

The drive home took a little longer than usual, and police cars were flashing red-and-blue lights everywhere. Michelle was more anxious to see what had happened than to know if she would return to work tomorrow or not.

BREAKING NEWS, the local channel's chyron said, *TERROR ATTACK INSIDE THE RENCEN BUILDING.*

"*. . .with a backpack, targeted more likely than not the Kirk's Brokerage office on the thirty-third floor,*" said the news anchor at the studio, in what sounded like a comment on what the reporter had said, "*What do we know about the attacker, his motive, and whether he had any connections with a terror group, was he on any watch-list et cetera?*"

"*Lisa, I spoke with officer Tad Brown, who sounded overwhelmed with the recent attacks in the city. He said that the attacker was a naturalized U.S. citizen, born and raised overseas. He did not reveal his name yet, but he said that he was caught on multiple security cameras and that, listen to this, they had a tip from his own family minutes before the attack happened. He said that his own mother had called 9-1-1 the moment she learned that the terrorist was planning the attack, but it was too late . . .*"

Michelle's phone rang.

"I quit," was the only thing she said after a moment of sober silence, after which she hung up.

A Railroad in Dearborn

Before she put the phone aside, she saw a text from a New York number that said "ARE YOU OK?" She remembered she had seen that number on her phone as she was corralled into the elevator.

XXV

"Ali, please, call my family!"

"My God, Sadiq, what happened to you?" said the cashier at Al-Yasmeen, upon seeing an unusually filthy Sadiq. He had obviously lost a few pounds, he wasn't shaved, and he was weak. Running from Stanley's had used up what was left of his stamina.

"Long story. I have no ride, no phone, my wallet is gone and it had all my papers, and I haven't eaten enough for a long time. Please, let Layla come pick me up," Sadiq was breathless.

"I will. Calm down. Nora, lead him to the sitting area and show him where the restrooms are," Ali said as he took his phone out of his pocket.

Sadiq was scanning the place like he'd been followed. He was not comforted by the late-morning crowd, nor by the presence of his friends who worked there. He was panting loudly but the place's noise was even louder. The only people who noticed him were Ali and Nora, and maybe the old

114

man who had just entered the restaurant and walked very confidently to the only empty table.

Sadiq washed up and left the restroom. He saw that he had to share a table with the lonely old man who was reading a paper at one end. Nora gave him a confirmation smile, and Sadiq proceeded to the other end of the table.

Less than a minute later, Nora came back with a glass of water for Sadiq, and told him that Ali had called Layla and left a voice message. "Tell him to call her again until he gets her, will you?"

Nora did not take Sadiq's imperative language personally. In fact, she felt sorry for him. "I will."

Sadiq thought that she paid more attention to the man sitting at the other end, which made the rest of his time at that table more awkward, so he picked up another paper and tried to read. The place was too loud though even for anyone to see the breaking news on the silent TV screen that was covering the source of the blast most of them had heard, so Sadiq threw the paper aside.

And yet, the TV screen was the first thing he saw afterward: BREAKING NEWS, TERROR ATTACK AT KIRK'S BROKERAGE.

Sadiq followed the news subtitle over and over again until Layla arrived. The old man reading the newspaper sensed the emotional scene and saw an excited, crying Layla running toward an indifferent, miserable Sadiq. He quietly observed from his end of the table.

"Where were you? Who was he? How did you get out? Wait, let's go home first. Mom doesn't believe it still. She'll be thrilled to see you!"

"Let's go. Give me the keys." Layla was surprised at the request but handed the keys to Sadiq anyway.

In case the whole restaurant was not watching the emotional reunion, Sadiq snatched the keys and ran all the way to the car. By the time Layla realized that her own brother had left her in the restaurant without a ride, it was too late.

XXVI

Falah woke up on a carpeted floor in a room that wasn't much cleaner than the basement, with the sun directly gleaming through a large window on his eyes. When he turned away from it, he saw Stanley sitting on an old couch trying to call someone.

Stanley was looking at Falah as he was waiting for an answer that did not come.

"Listen to me, young man. If you or your family try to pull a fast one on me, I will hunt you all one by one. Do you understand me?"

"Yes. Sir." Falah's voice was too tired to show the sarcasm. "Have they not answered you?"

"By the end of today, if your father doesn't answer, you'll take me to their place if you want to live." At least Falah was now pretty sure he was not moved for a summary execution, although he couldn't believe the request he had just heard.

"My family is too poor," he said to Stanley. "You may want to go easy on them.

118

A Railroad in Dearborn

They would've already given you what you wanted if they could."

"We'll see how poor they are . . ." The conversation was interrupted by Falah's phone ringing. "Yes?"

Long pause. Stanley's face was attentive. Falah's heart managed to have enough energy to race like base drum mallets pounding on his chest.

"No no no, wait. I'll call and let you know where. Is that clear?" Falah wasn't any less anxious.

"Good. Keep your phone next to you." Stanley hung up and addressed Falah again.

"You better hope this goes well, young man. Just a couple more days and you'll either walk out of this place free or delivered to your family in a plastic bag. I'll get you something to eat. Don't die on me before that."

XXVII

"That boy sure runs fast for someone who hasn't eaten much."

Layla wasn't interested in making a small conversation with the uninvited old man at the beginning, until she realized what he had just said. Layla turned to him, frowning.

"How did you know he hasn't eaten much?" There was a split-second in which Layla thought that he was the kidnapper, before she remembered that he shared the table with her brother, and that he didn't sound anything like the kidnapper on the phone.

"I know some Arabic. This is Dearborn, isn't it? I heard him talking with the guy at the front.

"I'm Kirk." By now, the dumbfounded Layla was already feeling confident toward the man, who had a calming voice.

"Nice to meet you," Layla said, a bit cautiously. "I don't know what's going on.

A Railroad in Dearborn

We were told that my brother was kidnapped. We were about to pay the kidnapper the ransom money he wanted, and now, I don't know what's going on. I don't know. I left my phone in my purse, and my purse in the car. I need a ride home now."

"I'll take you home if you want."

"No, thank you. Ali will." Apparently, Layla didn't trust the man enough to leave the restaurant with him.

"Why didn't you call the police instead?"

"You're kidding, aren't you? What would the police do? When was the last time you saw a police car crossing these tracks?"

"I don't blame you. Dearborn has changed a lot."

"It's that Kirk's Brokerage," Layla somehow thought she would feel better if she managed to insult the man by associating his name with the company.

"How?"

"The very company my brother was planning to work for is the reason behind his kidnapping. They said it used to work for the whole metropolis, but they somehow managed to segregate the Arabs from the city and the northern suburbs. They served every part of the north, no part on this side of the railroad. That side went up, ours went down until it became irreversible crime-ridden, and the worst may not be here yet."

"The plan was to love all and to serve all," Kirk said.

"That's what they what you to think."

"Trust me."

"I'm in no mood for debates, sir. I'm just waiting for my ride home now."

"I'm Kirk."

"I know. You just said that." It took Layla a second to notice that the man gestured toward the TV screen that was still covering the bombing. She thought it's best for her to stay silent and see where the man goes with this.

A Railroad in Dearborn

"My father was a successful stockbroker at Wall Street. I inherited all his money and assets after he passed away, being his only son. I had a burning desire to serve the poor, and my biggest opportunity was Detroit. The city, the whole metropolis was miserable. Filthy. Businesses were closing and the fortunate people were leaving.

"I quit my work in New York and came here, not seeking any profit except to see people happy. I established the company to invest in the city. I flipped houses with a financial loss, volunteered to renovate the city's blocks, and yet I always managed to have enough resources.

"I loaned money to those who couldn't borrow from banks. New immigrants and people with bad credit. Those who could pay back, did. Those who couldn't, I forgave their debts.

"I was diligent to write the company's bylaws in a way that makes it a continuous mission for it to help the poor, to serve people on both sides of the tracks. I left the company under the leadership of a competent board. I trusted the CEO with the stewardship of this work, to equally serve all and to ensure the spirit of love and sacrifice in the workplace, even though I knew that I couldn't trust them forever.

"And I was right. The company was given to greed. Its staff, to prejudice. The salt of the earth lost its savor. I've been silently watching its performance and I still wonder how they managed to survive when they drifted that far from their original path. How do they expect to continue when they stand for hate, instead of love, I don't know.

"All I know is that I founded a company on love, only to be hated by the very ones I sacrificed everything to serve, because of my own company's staff. I'm sorry this is happening to you, Layla, but this is not my fault.

"And I promise you that, even though I've been away for two decades, it won't take long for me to restore your community, and my company, and to reward those who walked right in it, and to make those responsible pay for their mistakes."

"You're ready, Layla?" came Ali's sound from the front.

124

A Railroad in Dearborn

Layla's eyes were frozen on Kirk's.

Wissam Youssif

XXVIII

"WHO IS THERE," was Michelle's text reply to the New York number that asked about her.

As she waited for the response, Travis called.

"Hi Travis, what's going on." Michelle and Travis knew each other long enough for him to know if anything had been wrong with her from the way she sounded, but by that time her voice was stable and monotonic.

"Tom called. Did you really quit?"

"I did. I'm glad he took it seriously enough he didn't wait till tomorrow to let you know."

"Why did you, Michelle? You want to let me do all the work by myself now? It's like the whole company depends on you!"

"No you won't. Tom is already on his way back. And besides, I cannot take this anymore. What's happening in our company is evil. Tom's racism is unchecked and Paul knows that. I feel guilty toward all those poor
126

people we let down. Dearborn is going down and Detroit will pay. No one on this side of the railroad will be safe and it's all because of our policies. My goodness our hate overflows everywhere. Tom doesn't . . ." at which point her voice disappeared for a while, followed by a snuffle, after which she continued in a higher voice, "Haven't you seen them? What's their fault?"

"I honestly stand with Tom."

"Travis!"

"Michelle I'm tired of your romantic ideals. You put love above our security. You think those animals across the railroad would love you back while they try to kill you every day. I've been blessed by Kirk's Brokerage that cares for me too much to not return that care to it and to my community, and I've been waiting for a guy like Tom to be in charge for too long already. Tom says it as it is because he doesn't want us all to get killed. You wouldn't understand because you're not from here. If you don't like things to be done the way they're done, you may want to move back to Boise. Don't you dream of seeing Kirk once again. He's dead.

Dead! And even if he's not, you'll be happy that you're not among us any more when he returns, 'cause you won't stay for very long in this company anyway."

"Tom has already appointed you for my place, hasn't he?"

"Not your place anymore. Anyway, I wish you all the best in your life."

Michelle was so dumbfounded she didn't even realize that Travis has hung up. By the time she looked at her phone screen, she saw a text from the New York number: "CALL ME."

Not a single man that Michelle met on dating websites was nice enough to wait for her to call him. Her thumb hovered over the number for a minute with her mind listing all the possibilities. Scam, emergency, stalker and so on, but no good news.

She pressed the call button. The phone rang once, and then a voice said:

"Hi Michelle, this is Kirk."

A Railroad in Dearborn

XXIX

Stanley was paralyzed with fear when he heard the knock on his door that Friday morning. He had been living alone for over a year and everyone had seen the angry "No Soliciting" and "No Trespassing" signs that kept even the Jehovah's Witnesses away from him.

The police car was visible through the living room's window.

Stanley wasn't prepared for that scenario, but he did manage to lift up the quiet, unresisting Falah into his bedroom and shut the door. "Not a word my friend, okay?"

Falah nodded.

"Good morning," was the only friendly thing the police officer said. "I'm Mark Haddad from the Dearborn Police Department. Is this Altima yours?"

"Yes, it is."

"We have a report on a stolen car that has a similar description. Would you mind showing us some papers?"

"No problem. They're in the glove compartment."

"Okay," the officer said. Stanley still couldn't believe this was happening, and he knew that he couldn't bluff for too long.

"Now, please. Let's go."

"I think they're inside."

"Take your time. We'll need the title and registration and also your driver's license. Hurry up, will you."

Stanley went back inside. He froze in the middle of the living room. His eyes were blank, and his mind had nothing to scan. Could he have avoided this trap had he killed Sadiq? Maybe his family as well? Could he have done that anyway?

The knock on his door stopped him from what might have been an endless series of possibilities.

"Mind if we come inside for a minute?"

"Yes, sure."

A Railroad in Dearborn

"What's your name?

"Stanley."

"Full name, please?"

Another officer was walking toward the bedroom.

And that's when Stanley pulled his Glock and shot the officer that was talking to him, who collapsed immediately. The second officer didn't get the chance to pull up his gun, and Stanley shot him in the head.

Everything happened so fast that Stanley had no time to digest the mess he has just made: there was a police car at his door, in a city that hadn't seen many police cars for years. There were two dead officers on his floor, whose carpet started to soak with their blood, their radios were crackling and beeping more rapidly, and his ransom money was supposed to be due that same morning.

"We're getting out of here," said Stanley as he lifted Falah from his bedroom's floor, the shock in whose withered eyes was obvious as he saw the conclusion of the gun shot sounds he had just heard. Stanley didn't feel Falah's weight as he turned back to the kitchen pantry and picked up a few large trash bags.

Falah's eyes opened wider.

"Don't worry, young man. Now relax while I put you in here. This is only till I get you to the car. I'll keep it open for you to breathe." Stanley said, as he started to stuff Falah into the bag, legs first.

As he opened the door, he realized that the police car was blocking his own car and that the only car available was the Altima. He turned back inside, still carrying Falah wrapped in trash bags and slung over his shoulder. Stanley picked up the Altima's keys and Falah's phone, went out and opened the trunk.

"One noise and you won't see your family," he warned, then placed Falah into the trunk.

Stanley then shut the trunk, got into the car, backed up, made a three-point turn and calmly drove up Chase Road toward Warren Avenue.

A Railroad in Dearborn

As he approached the railroad intersection the warning lights began to signal. He accelerated as the train was approaching from the right. He barely missed the train,

before a police car appeared, out of nowhere, on his rearview mirror.

He continued to drive at the same speed even as the police car was flashing its red and blue, and the Dearborn late-morning traffic didn't make it any easier for him. The police car sounded its siren as Stanley turned right into Junction Street, and it looked like the cop car was continuously rear-ending the Altima.

Stanley floored it as he turned left into Michigan Avenue, and the police car was joined by two others, sounding their sirens. Panicked drivers watched curiously as they opened the way for the wild chase. Stanley slowed down as he approached the old Train Station.

At the old building's gate, Stanley parked the Altima, while half a dozen angry police officers scrambled with aimed guns from their vehicles:

"Step out of the car and put your hands in the air!"

"C'mon! Get out!" Two officers started inching toward the Altima.

"Stay where you are! I have a hostage! You move, he dies!" Stanley's confident voice was the loudest in Roosevelt Park that morning.

The police officers froze, still pointing their guns toward Stanley.

"I'm serious! One move and an innocent, good citizen dies!"

Stanley popped up the trunk and slowly opened the door. Falah raised his head, desperate for the air he was gasping. Stanley pointed his gun toward Falah and was in total control of the situation.

"Let's go, young man!" With the old Train Station at his back, Stanley was surveying the Roosevelt Park that was littered with the officers and their vehicles. He slowly walked back into the abandoned

134

A Railroad in Dearborn

Train Station like he knew it by heart. Once inside, he hid behind a wall and sprinted toward the paneless window on the right of the entrance. He seized Falah with his left arm as he pulled Falah's phone from his right pocket and dialed Falah's father.

"Yeah, it's me. I need you to come over to the old Train Station with the cash. *Now.*"

By the time he hung up, a voice came from the bullhorn speaker at the Roosevelt Park. A SWAT truck was now parked outside.

"Come out of the property with your hands in the air. Now!"

Stanley gave Falah a desperate push that knocked him to the filthy floor. The fear in Falah's eyes pleaded with Stanley as he pulled out his Glock:

"It's over, buddy."

BANG!

And that's when Stanley, to Falah's surprise, fell down, to reveal an old man in a polo shirt behind him. Stanley's head hit Kirk's boots, and his eyes went blank.

A Railroad in Dearborn

XXX

"IT TAKES A GOOD GUY WITH A GUN

TO TAKE DOWN A BAD GUY WITH A GUN," said the Facebook meme that had Kirk's first revealed picture, as Michelle was scrolling down her social media account on her phone, waiting for the local news in the afternoon of that crisp day in late October. Her smile mingled with warm tears as she looked into the eyes of the owner and CEO of her company.

With the TV on mute, she didn't realize that the news had already started. She glanced up from her phone and read the subtitles, not even thinking to turn on the sound.

"Detroit Militia member charged with multiple counts of murder related to Riverside Park birthday massacre in July.

"Dearborn resident among 11 arrested in raid on Detroit Militia cell.

"Sadiq Jafar, 23, had been kidnapped by notorious Stanley William, police say.

"Kirk's Brokerage wins bid to build and operate Detroit-Dearborn street car."

And that's when Michelle's phone rang. The caller's name drew a charming smile on her lips as she answered with a slow and quiet "Heyyy! How is Mr. Falah doing this afternoon?"

"Always fine when Miss Michelle is fine! Even better if she would go out for dinner with me on Sunday evening!"

"You know I go to church on Sunday evening!" Michelle was still smiling. She was sure she could hear Falah's smile thorough his voice.

"Is it okay if I come with you?"